Buffy the Vampire Slayer™

Pale Reflections

PALE REFLECTIONS

based on the television series created by
JOSS WHEDON

writer **ANDI WATSON**

"Killing Time" written by **DOUG PETRIE**

penciller **CLIFF RICHARDS**

inker **JOE PIMENTEL**

colorist **GUY MAJOR**

letterer **AMADOR CISNEROS**

cover art **DAVE STEWART**

These stories take place during Buffy the Vampire Slayer's third season.

TITAN BOOKS

publisher
MIKE RICHARDSON

editor
SCOTT ALLIE
with **ADAM GALLARDO**

collection designer
KEITH WOOD

art director
MARK COX

special thanks to
DEBBIE OLSHAN AT FOX LICENSING,
CAROLINE KALLAS AND GEORGE SNYDER AT *BUFFY THE VAMPIRE SLAYER*,
AND DAVID CAMPITI AT GLASS HOUSE GRAPHICS.

Buffy the Vampire Slayer™: Pale Reflections. Published by Titan Books a division of Titan Publishing Group Ltd., by arrangement with Dark Horse Comics, Inc.

PUBLISHED BY
TITAN BOOKS
144 SOUTHWARK STREET
LONDON SE1 0UP

what did you think of this book? we love to hear from our readers.
please e-mail us at readerfeedback@titanemail.com or write to
Reader Feedback at the address above.

FIRST EDITION
DECEMBER 2000
ISBN: 1 - 84023 - 236 - 6

3 5 7 9 10 8 6 4 2

print valprint in italy.

introduction

Buffy Summers's senior year has been plagued by zombie models and high-octane vampires. Behind it all has been one unseen hand: Selke, a vampire Buffy almost killed over a year ago, on Halloween. The same alchemical experiments which led to the super-powered vampires have now produced Selke's ultimate secret weapon – a perfect clone of the Slayer. As the town prepares for a huge outdoor festival and parade, Buffy, Angel, and the Scooby Gang must get to the heart of Sunnydale's Bad Blood problem.

Art by JEFF MATSUDA *and* JON SIBAL
Colors by GUY MAJOR

YOUR CHEATIN' HEART

YOU GOT ALL THAT?

D'UH, LIKE YOU'LL LET ME FORGET. FIRST--KILL BUFFY. SECOND--MAKE HER FRIENDS SUFFER LIKE SHE MADE YOUR FRIENDS SUFFER.
WELL DONE, HONEY. NOW YOU DO THIS LITTLE THING FOR US AND WE'LL BE VERY PLEASED.
THAT'S RIGHT, NOW--
PLEASED ENOUGH TO GIVE ME A CLOTHES ALLOWANCE?
YES, YES, YOU CAN HAVE ALL THE CLOTHES YOU WANT AFTER YOU'VE DONE YOUR CHORES.
YOU RUN ALONG NOW AND CALL IF YOU'RE GOING TO BE LATE.
KIDS. YOU BRING 'EM INTO THE WORLD AND ALL THEY DO IS TAKE, TAKE, TAKE.

--BUT WHAT KIND OF FLOAT SHOULD WE BUILD?
USE YOUR INITIATIVE.SOMETHING THAT EXEMPLIFIES THE QUALITIES OF SUNNYDALE HIGH.

DO WE HAVE ENOUGH RAZOR WIRE FOR A STALAG?

WHY DOES HE ALWAYS PICK ON US?
IT'S HIS WAY OF SHOWING AFFECTION.

HE'S AN EVIL GENIUS. WHO ELSE COULD TAKE ALL THE FUN OUT OF MARDI GRAS?
SO, SUGGESTIONS FOR THE FLOAT DESIGN.

A PINK FLUFFY BUNNY?
A HOLE BELCHING GORE AND FLAMES WITH DEMONS SPILLING OUT?

AND A GOOD MORNING TO YOU TOO.
SORRY, GILES. WE'R FULL OF FLOA HATE.

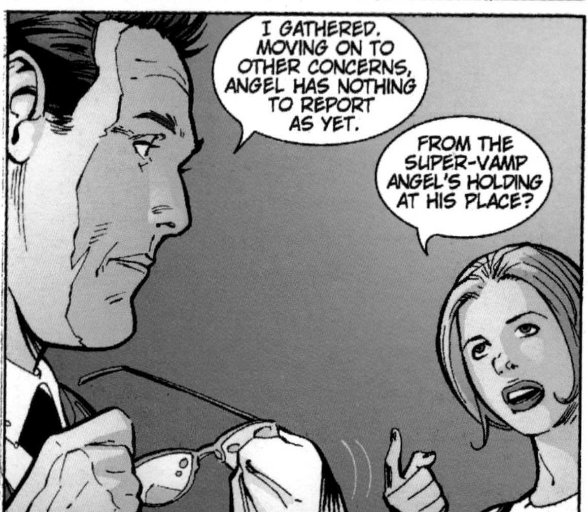
I GATHERED. MOVING ON TO OTHER CONCERNS, ANGEL HAS NOTHING TO REPORT AS YET.
FROM THE SUPER-VAMP ANGEL'S HOLDING AT HIS PLACE?

YES. IT SEEMS HE'S QUITE A STUBBORN FELLOW, BUT ANGEL'S SURE HE WILL PROVIDE US WITH SOME INFORMATION SOON.
LIKE WHERE THESE" SUPER-VAMPS" CAME FROM?

INDEED. EACH NIGHT BRINGS MORE CHAOS AND WE HAVEN'T A CLUE HOW IT STARTED...
HOW ABOUT A GIANT GRINNING CLOWN?

UGH, CLOWNS.

ANYTIME YOU WANT TO TALK--

NOTHING TO SAY TO YOU.

SURE.

GUESS WHAT KIND OF WATER IS IN THIS PISTOL?

ARE YOU SURE YOU DON'T WANT A LIFT.
I'LL RUN HOME WHILE I HAVE THE ENERGY TO BURN.
IF YOU'RE SURE--
CLIFF'S
OOH, NICE OUTFIT.
HOMEWORK FIRST.

A TOAST TO A DEAD SLAYER.
SMASH
TASTES LIKE HELL.
SOMETHING ISN'T RIGHT.

DON'T BE PARANOID, BUFFY.
SKRASHHH
READY FOR YOUR WORKOUT?

LET ME KNOW IF I GO TOO FAST FOR YOU.
RRIPPP
OH, I WILL.
SLOW.
PREDICTABLE.
Y'SEE, I KNOW YOUR NEXT MOVE BEFORE YOU DO.

B-BU--
SURPRISE!
DIDN'T SEE IT COMIN', HUH?
WE LOOK THE SAME, BUT YOUR REPARTEE SUCKS.

DIDN'T SEE THAT COMIN', HUH?
WOH-OH.
SLIPPERY WHEN WET.
OOF!

LET ME HELP YOU UP.

THIS IS NO TIME FOR STYLING, BUFFY.

ARRRGGH!

ARRRGH!
I'M GONNA KILL YOU FOR THAT.
GASP GASP
GASP
WE'VE DONE YOUR HAIR, TIME FOR YOUR NAILS.

WORLD'S WORST SHOT.
MY FACE!? NOOOO!
YOU'RE SO DEAD!
IF I HAD A QUARTER FOR EVERY TIME I'VE HEARD THAT.

IF THIS DOESN'T KILL YOU--
--I'LL GIVE YOU THE--

--QUARTER.
DEAD. ALMOST TOO EASY.
MIRROR!
B-BUT--

GOTTA FIND THE DOC. HE CAN HELP ME.

SKRRRRRR

SKRRRRRR

SPLASH

DOC-- DOC! HELP ME!
WHAT HAPPENED? WAS IT BUFFY?

I'LL BE PRETTY, RIGHT? I'LL STILL BE BEAUTIFUL?
THERE'LL BE NO SCARS?
N-NO. I'LL... I'LL--

I'LL BE PERFECT.
I HAVEN PERFORM SURGERY F SOME TIME, B I HAVEN'T LO MY TOUC

THIS MAY STING A LITTLE.
DOC, WHY CAN'T I SEE MYSELF IN THE MIRROR?

IT MUST BE YOUR VAMPIRE BLOOD...CASTS NO REFLECTION.
THAT'S SO UNFAIR.

YES, TOO BAD THE ONE YOU LOVE THE MOST CANNOT SEE YOU.
DID BUFFY DO THIS TO YOU?

YES. I BARELY HAD TIME TO KILL HER BEFORE RUSHING OVER HERE--

TELETUBBIES?

DON'T THINK SO.
HOW ABOUT SOMETHING MORE EXOTIC--
I COULD BE A SULTAN, AND YOU, WILLOW, AND BUFFY COULD BE MY HAREM.
NOT EVEN IN YOUR DREAMS.

HEY, GUYS. WHTCHA DOIN'?
DEFINITELY IN MY DREAMS.

OH WOW, ANNA SUI?
SINCE WHEN DID YOU KNOW THE DIFFERENCE BETWEEN WALMART AND A DESIGNER LABEL?

WE'RE STILL TRYING TO COME UP WITH A CONCEPT FOR THIS FLOAT.
YEAH, THAT'S TOO BAD.
SO, WHERE *DID* YOU GET THAT OUTFIT?
OH, BUFFY. WHAT HAPPENED TO YOUR FACE?

DON'T EVER TOUCH ME!

BUFFY!
THAT WASN'T COOL.
BUFF, IF YOU'RE AUDITIONING FOR "MOOD SW POSTER GIRL YOU'VE GOT THE PART.
I'M SORRY- I'VE BEEN KIND OF WOUND UP LATELY.

I'D SAY YOU WERE SPRUNG.
NO, REALLY, BUFFY, IT'S OKAY.

HEY--WHY DON'T I HELP YOU WITH AN IDEA FOR THE FLOAT?
THAT'D BE GREAT, BUFFY.

HOW ABOUT...

4 FUN
...CLOWNS!
CLOWNS?
YEAH, IT COULD BE A CLOWN STICKING OUT HIS TONGUE SO IT LOOKS LIKE A SLIDE,AND A LITTLE GIRL COULD BE SLIDING DOWN.
CLOWNS?
AFTER ALL...
...EVERYBODY LOVES A CLOWN.
TECHNICALLY, NOT *EVERYBODY* LOVES A CLOWN.
THIS IS GOING TO BE GREAT!
YEAH, A REAL SCREAM.

ARRGHHHH!
GIMME BLOOD, I'M BEGGING YOU.
TELL ME AND I MIGHT LET YOU GO.
IT'S REGULAR STRENGTH, BUT IT'S YOURS.
I DON'T KNOW WHERE THE NEW BLOOD CAME FROM. I JUST KNOW THERE'S A WOMAN AND SOME KIND OF SURGEON.
THEY CONTROL THE BLOOD AND RULE THE NEW VAMPIRES.
A SURGEON? THAT'S NOTHING TO GO ON...

IT'S ALL I GOT--HEY, WHERE YOU GOIN'!?
HEYYY!

Art by JEFF MATSUDA *and* JON SIBAL
Colors by GUY MAJOR

SHE'S
NO LADY

HI!
GOT I.D.?
I.D.?
NO I.D., NO DEAL. THAT'S OUR POLICY.
YOU DON'T EVEN KNOW WHAT I WANT YET!

YOU WANT TO GO HOME TO MOMMY AND GET YOUR I.D., OR COME BACK IN A COUPLE OF YEARS.
RA
OH, JEEZU--
DON'T YOU EVER--
--EVER TOUCH M
I MOM

LOOK WHAT YOU DID--
--YOU 'ROID RIDDEN FREAK!
WHAT THE--I'M CALLING THE COPS!
MOMMY.

YOU'LL GROW FINS IF YOU STAY IN THERE ANY LONGER.
JUST A SEC.

I HAVE TO GO, BUFFY.

STUPID MIRRORS... WHAT GOOD--

URGHH!

MY, YOU HAVE BEEN WORKING DILIGENTLY.
IF THAT MEANS HARD, THEN YEAH.

WE'RE A LITTLE CLOSER TO FINDING THE ORIGIN OF THESE DREADFUL NEW VAMPIRES. ANGEL HAS DISCOVERED A LEAD INVOLV--WHERE'S BUFFY?
SHE'S LATE... AGAIN.

WHAT DO YOU MEAN, AGAIN?
EVER SINCE SHE BECAME STEPFORD BUFFY.

SHE HASN'T BEEN HERSELF LATELY.
HOW EXACTLY?

OH, LISTEN TO YOU PARANOIDS. THE GIRL TAKES AN INTEREST IN HER APPEARANCE FOR ONCE AND DO YOU ENCOURAGE HER? NO.

OF COURSE, HER SUDDEN INTEREST IN FASHION WAS NEW TO ME. BUT THEN I THOUGHT, WHAT'S THE SURPRISE? SHE SPENDS MOST OF HER TIME RAMMING STAKES THROUGH THE UNDEAD.
Y'SEE? FASHION, CORDY DEFENDING BUFFY. "WE HAVE ENTERED A NEW DIMENSION . . ."
YES, HAVE HER COME SEE ME. DON'T LIKE WHERE IS GOING. THE SITU IS TOO SERIOUS F THE SLAYER TO G CORDY.
HEY, I RESENT THAT.
YOU WERE SAYING, ABOUT ANGEL?
YES. IT SEEMS THERE'S A CONNECTION BETWEEN A FEMALE VAMPIRE AND A SURGEON. I'M INVESTIGATING THE LOCAL HOSPITALS, BLOOD SPECIALISTS BEING THE FIRST POINT OF ENQUIRY.
WHAT ARE WE SEARCHING FOR?
I DON'T KNOW. UNUSUAL AREAS OF RESEARCH, KEEPING LATE HOURS...? I REALLY DON'T KNOW. ANGEL IS QUESTIONING HIS UNDERGROUND CONTACTS. TOGETHER WE HOPE TO FIND SOMETHING.
I CAN HELP AFTER SCHOOL.
MUCH APPRECIATED. BUT UNTIL THEN CONCENTRATE ON FINISHING THIS--
--WORK OF . . . ART.

--DOUBLE MOCHA--
--WHIPPED CREAM AND CHOCOLATE SPRINKLES... PLEASE--

I DON'T WANT TO BE A CLOWN.
WHY NOT?

BECAUSE I'LL LOOK SILLY.
ISN'T THAT THE POINT?
I THINK WE'LL ALL LOOK PRET COOL.

YOU DWEEBS DON'T HAVE A REPUTATION LIKE MINE TO UPHOLD.
NO COMMENT.

ALL RIGHT! IF IT'LL MAKE YOU HAPPY TAKE MINE.
VERY FUNNY.

GOOD GRIEF!
GOOD AFTERNOON, BUFFY. NICE OF YOU TO JOIN US.

WHAT!? I HAVEN'T BEEN FEELING TOO GOOD, OKAY?
WELL, YOU'RE JUST IN TIME FOR DRESS REHEARSAL.

OH, SO SHE GETS THE GOOD COSTUME.
WHAT'S SO GOOD ABOUT IT?
IT MAKES HER LOOK THIN!
BUFFY, WHAT'S THE PROBLEM?
NOTHING! JUST-- SLAYER STUFF.
C'MON, BUFFY. DON'T HOLD OUT ON ME. WE SHARE, REMEMBER?
I'M FINE, OKAY!?
I'VE TRIED ON YOUR STUPID COSTUME, NOW I HAVE MORE IMPORTANT THINGS TO DO!
HEY, BUFFY, GILES WANTS TO SEE YOU RIGHT AWAY.
MEE-OWWW! WHO PUT HER CYCLE IN A SPIN?

WOH-OH!
KRUNCH
BITE ME!
TELL ME.
TELL ME.
THE GUY, THEY CALL HIM DOC B-BUT HE HAS A CLINIC. D-DOC FLITTER OR SOMETHING.
THANKS FOR THE TIP.

FULL OF TINY... METALLIC FRAGMENTS?
THAT WAS NEVER PART OF MY FORMULA.
THEY'VE BEEN ADDED AFTER THE FACT.
WHICH MIGHT EXPLAIN--
WHERE IS SHE!?
SHE NEVER CALLS HER MOTHER.

I'VE BEEN WORRIED SICK.
ERR, THERE, THERE. DON'T YOU WORRY, I'M SURE SHE'LL COME RIGHT THROUGH THAT DOOR WITH THE SLAYER'S CORPSE ANY MINUTE NOW.
YOU DON'T KNOW THAT.

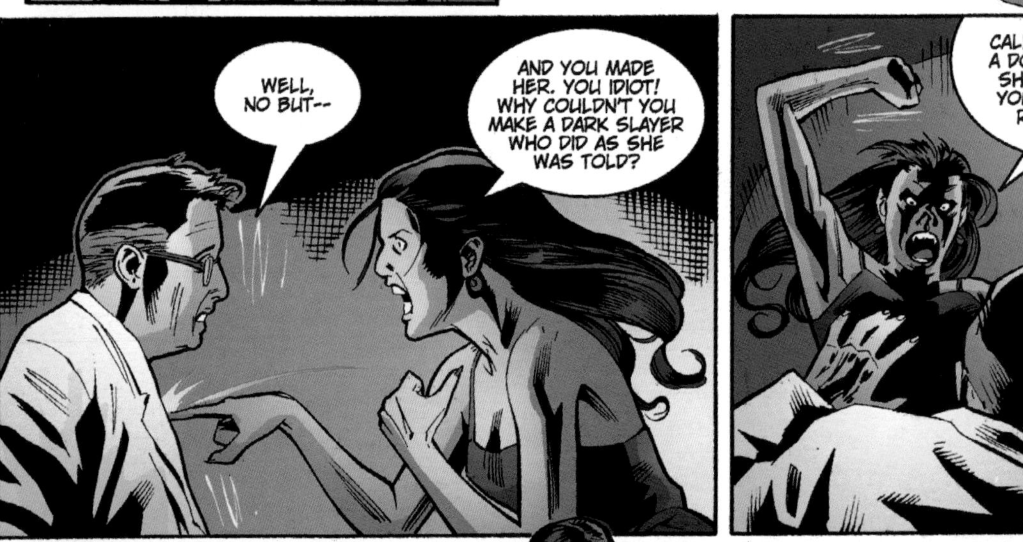
WELL, NO BUT--
AND YOU MADE HER. YOU IDIOT! WHY COULDN'T YOU MAKE A DARK SLAYER WHO DID AS SHE WAS TOLD?
CALL YOURSELF A DOCTOR? YOU SHOULD HAVE YOUR LICENSE REVOKED.

S-SORRY, MISTRESS. CREATING THE EMBODIMENT OF EVIL WITH GOOD MANNERS IS A DIFFICULT TASK.
EXCUSES, EXCUSES! THAT'S ALL I EVER HEAR.

IF YOU WANT A JOB DONE WELL... COME ON! WE'RE GOING TO FIND YOUR DARK SLAYER.

-YAWN-
FINISHED, FINALLY.
WHAT THE--
BUFFY?
CABOOM

ALL PLAY AND NO WORK--
URK!
--MAKES THE DARK SLAYER A GREASE SPOT UNDER MY HEEL.
I... -GACK- DONE MY... CHORES.
WELL, MISSY, IF BUFFY IS DEAD, WHERE'S HER CORPSE?
I'M SURE SHE HAS IT SOMEWHERE, MISTRESS.
YEAH, I KILLED HER, BUT I DIDN'T KEEP THE BODY. THINK I'M SOME KIND OF SICKO?
YESSS!

SHE'S DEAD, DOC.
SHE'S DEAADD!
AAHHH. IT'S LIKE SOME HUGE WEIGHT HAS BEEN LIFTED OFF MY SHOULDERS. I'M SO HAPPY.
THAT'S WONDERFUL, MISTRESS.
NOW, WHERE DID YOU PUT THE BODY?
I DUMPED IT IN THE SEWERS.
OF COURSE YOU DID. NOW GO FIND THE REMAINS AND BRING THEM TO ME.
WE CAN'T THROW A PARTY WITHOUT A BODY. WHEN YOU KILL A SLAYER YOU HAVE TO CELEBRATE!
HERE YOU GO. NOW RUN ALONG ...
WELL, DOC, PARTY PREPARATIONS. DO YOU HAVE A FAVORITE KIND OF JELLO?

improved blood ?roves
intensely addictive
side effects? poisoned?
SO NICE OF YOU TO BREAK IN.
I'M GONNA POP YOU LIKE A ZIT, PRETTY BOY.

CREAAAK
KRAK
WHA--!?

OWWWW.
A POISONED CHALICE.

KRASSH

EAT. YOU'VE BEEN UNDER FOR TWO DAYS.
OOF. FEELS LIKE I'VE BEEN UNDER A BUS.
WHO ARE YOU?
I'M A SISTER.
YOU'RE ...ME?

A MIRROR IMAGE MADE BY SELKE AND THE DOCTOR.
SELKE? SHE'S BEHIND THIS? I THOUGHT SHE WAS TOAST.
SHE WANTS YOU DEAD.
SO SHE SENT MY OTHER EVIL TWIN TO KILL ME?
I WAS AN EARLY FAILURE.
YOU DON'T SEEM TO HAVE ACCEPTED YOUR MISSION.
I WAS DUMPED BY THEM AND LEFT FOR DEAD.
BUT WHY SAVE ME?
I'M DYING. I WANT YOU TO LIVE. WHEN YOU'RE WELL, YOU WILL GO BACK AND KILL THEM.
I APPRECIATE YOU DRAGGING ME OUT OF THE DIRT AND EVERYTHING, BUT I'M BARELY UP TO SPEED WITH THE STORY SO FAR--
DON'T YOU WORRY YOUR PRETTY LITTLE HEAD, SIS--

--THIS IS WHERE THE STORY ENDS.
MACYS

Art by JEFF MATSUDA *and* JON SIBAL
Colors by GUY MAJOR

OLD FRIEND

SORRY TO HURRY YOU INTO ROUND TWO, BUT I HAVE NEW OUTFITS TO TRY ON.
HISSSSS
YOU FIRST-- THEN THE RUNT.
THAT'S NO WAY TO TALK ABOUT YOUR SISTER.
EVER HEAR OF SIBLING RIVALRY?
NNGTH!

IT'S BLOOD... BUT NOT LIKE I'VE EVER SEEN.
YOU'RE ABSOLUTELY SURE THAT THIS IS FROM "BUFFY"?
YEAH. SHE MUST HAVE CUT HERSELF INSIDE THE COSTUME.
I GUESS THIS IS GOOD NEWS?
THE BUFFY WE'VE BEEN SEEING ISN'T THE REAL BUFFY, BUT SOME KIND OF... FRANKEN-BUFFY.
WHICH EXPLAINS HER WEIRD BEHAVIOR.
I'VE BEEN HANGING OUT WITH A CHEAP KNOCK OFF?
IT WOULD BE GOOD NEWS IF WE KNEW WHERE THE REAL BUFFY IS.
ANOTHER THING IS--
TAKE A CLOSE LOOK AT THIS. I FOUND THE SOURCE OF THE NEW BLOODS.
IT WAS HOUSED IN A PLASTIC SURGERY CLINIC. THIS DOC FLITTER IS INVOLVED.

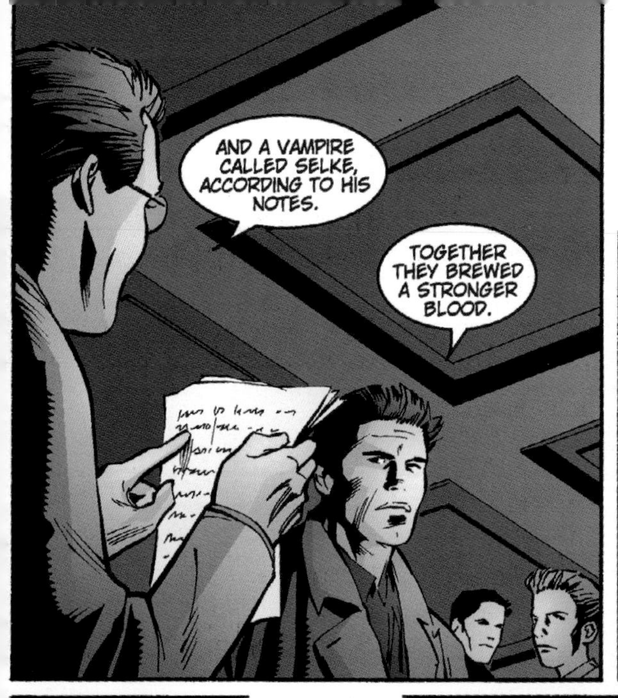
AND A VAMPIRE CALLED SELKE, ACCORDING TO HIS NOTES.
TOGETHER THEY BREWED A STRONGER BLOOD.

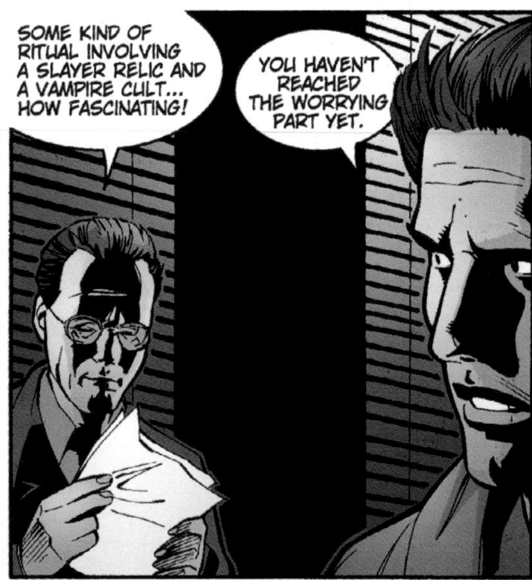
SOME KIND OF RITUAL INVOLVING A SLAYER RELIC AND A VAMPIRE CULT... HOW FASCINATING!
YOU HAVEN'T REACHED THE WORRYING PART YET.

IT'S FROM THE SAME SOURCE. THEY BREWED THE BLOOD AND MADE THE NAUGHTY BUFFY.
"NAUGHTY BUFFY"?

THE BLOOD IS POISONED!

THAT'S WHAT I WAS GONNA TELL YOU. THERE ARE METALLIC FRAGMENTS IN THE BLOOD. THE CELLS HAVE DEGENERATED AND MUTATED EVEN JUST WHILE I'VE BEEN STUDYING THEM.

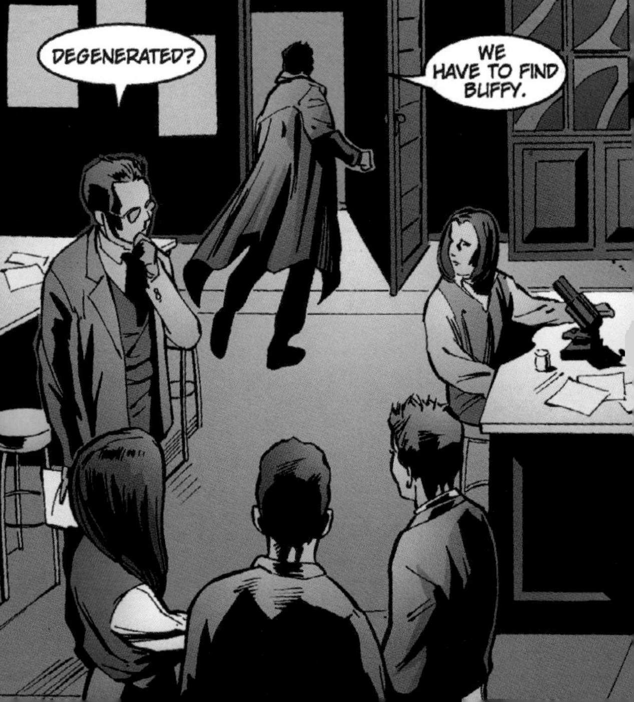
DEGENERATED?
WE HAVE TO FIND BUFFY.

STILL A LITTLE SORE FROM OUR LAST BOUT?
A LITTLE--
--HOW 'BOUT YOU?
WAH!
NOT A TWINGE.
YOU LOOK DIFFERENT--

--OLDER.
GRRR
I'M FINE. IT MUST BE YOUR EYESIGHT--
WOH-OH-OH!
--YOU CAN'T SEE STRAIGHT.
OOF!
YOU SEE STARS?
SLAP

--PARTY HATS, NAPKINS, AND ONE OF THOSE CLOWNS THAT MAKE POODLES OUT OF BALLOONS.
ERR, WONDERFUL IDEA, MISTRESS.

WHAT THE... NO.
VANDALS?

MY BLOOD, MY PRECIOUS BLOOD!
I...I'LL GO STRAIGHT AWAY TO...TO COLLECT INGREDIENTS TO RESTART BREWING.

WHO DID THIS? WHERE ARE MY GUARDS?!

I'LL TEAR THEM INTO STRIPS!

GRARRRR

MY... FACE.
YOU DON'T LOOK SO GOOD. YOU'RE DYING, LIKE YOUR SISTER.
I'LL WATCH YOU DIE FIRST.
NO, I INSIST--
--AFTER
OOF!

NO, "AFTER OOF."
A LITTLE PAYBACK.
ARRGH!
SPLOO

THIS TIME I'LL--
--FINISH THE JOB.
TOGETHER AT LAST.
UH?
THUD

DID YOU GUYS FIND ANYTHING?
NOPE. YOU NEITHER?

ANY NEWS?

NO. WHAT ABOUT ANGEL?
WE DIDN'T FIND HER. HE'S GONE UNDERGROUND TO CONTINUE HIS SEARCH.

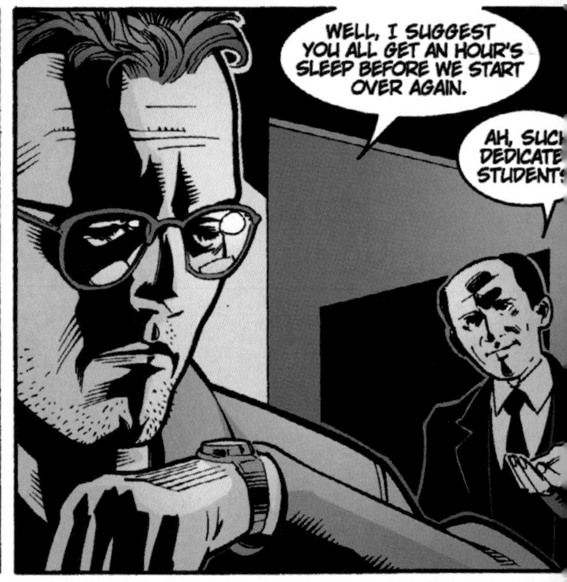
WELL, I SUGGEST YOU ALL GET AN HOUR'S SLEEP BEFORE WE START OVER AGAIN.
AH, SUC DEDICATE STUDENT

BURNING THE MIDNIGHT OIL TO HONOR OUR SCHOOL WITH THIS...UNIQUE FLOAT.

NO TIME FOR NAPPING. FRESHEN UP AND GET READY. THE PARADE STARTS IN LESS THAN AN HOUR.

D-DOC.
IF YOU TAKE THE EAST SIDE--
WHAT THE--
HMMM. THE VAMPIRE BLOOD. IT'S REACTING!
I DON'T KNOW WHAT THIS MEANS, BUT I'M SURE IT'S BAD.
GACCCKKKKK
PFF! SHOW-OFFS. THEY GET A GREAT COSTUME AND THINK THEY OWN THE PLACE.

GARRRRRR
WOOOO!
COOOOOL!
ARGGHHH
URR, GOTHS.
GRARRRRR
WHERE'D EVERYONE GO?
FOR A PERMANENT SWIM...
UNIVERSAL STUDIO'S MONSTER SHOW IS COOLER.
GRARRRRR
AIEEEE

CATCH!
GRARRRR
GAH
SKRAK
IT'S NOT YOUR NIGHT, HUH?
THUNK
OR YOURS.
KLONG
NOW *THAT* WAS COOL!

GACK
HURRY--
QUICK.
SNAP
ALLOW ME.
BUFFY?
IS THAT YOU?
THUNK
YOU GOT GOO UNDER THERE?
YOWCH!
THAT'S NO FAKE. IT'S MY BUFFY.
WHAT KIND OF HAPPY REUNION IS THAT?
BUFFY!

WE HAD AN ANTI-SOCIAL UNDERSTUDY REPLACE YOU FOR SOME TIME. WE FEARED THE WORST.
I TOOK CARE OF MY EVIL TWIN. ONE BUFFY IS ENOUGH.
THE NEW BLOODS ARE MUTATING INTO MONSTERS.
IT ALL STEMS FROM A VAMP CALLED SELKE. SHE BEARS A GRUDGE AGAINST--
BUFFY!

YOUR REPARTEE HASN'T IMPROVED.
GRARRRR
THWACK
WHERE'S THE WITTY COMEBACKS?
HAH!
RIGHT HERE.
T-WACK
OOF!
ice dream

BENSON'S & SONS
YOU GET MY COMIC BOOKS IF I DON'T MAKE IT.
THANKS, MAN.
COME AND GET IT-- WHOA! OH!
NEVER UNDERESTIMATE SLAPSTICK SHOES, UGLY.
GRAH
I KNEW I WOULDN'T LIKE YOU ANGRY.

I OWE YOU, MISSY.
I'M BUFFY, NOT MISSY.
WHATEVER, YOU'RE DEAD.
NO, I'M BUFFY. I ALMOST NEVER DIE.

KRUNCH
OH, REALLY?
REALLY.
NNNNGGGGGG
IT HAPPENS NOW AND AGAIN--
--BUT I ALWAYS COME BACK.
THIS TIME YOU WON'T RETURN.
NAH.

WHAP
JUST WHEN IT LOOKS LIKE IT'S ALL OVER--
WHAP
--I DRAW ON MY LAST RESERVES--
I COULD DO WITH A LITTLE HELP HERE.
POOOMF

--AND WIN IN THE END.
KRUNCH
POOOMF
POOOMF
POOOMF
MF

FASCINATING. THEY WERE BORN FROM HER WORK, AND DIED WITH HER. NOT A NORMAL VAMPIRE TRAIT, BUT NOT UNHEARD OF IN OTHER MAGICAL PRACTICES.
AND LUCKY FOR US.
SO, WHERE HAVE YOU BEEN LATELY, BUFF?
IN THE SEWER.
YOU CAN TAKE THE GIRL OUT OF THE SEWER--
I REALLY NEED A SHOWER. AND MY BED.
I HAVE MUCH FOLLOW-UP WORK TO DO ON THIS INCIDENT.
SIGH, THE PAPERWORK.
WELL, I'M JUST GLAD THIS THING'S BEHIND US. THERE'S ONLY ROOM FOR ONE BUFFY IN THIS TOWN.
THE END

Art by RANDY GREEN *and* ANDY OWENS
Colors by GUY MAJOR

KILLING
TIME

Buffy THE VAMPIRE SLAYER
KILLING TIME
TEN MINUTES AGO.
IS THIS LEGAL?

NO, IT'S STEALING. LOOK. THAT MUSEUM'S GOT LOTS OF STUFF--WHAT'S ONE MUSTY OLD NECKLACE?
YOU WANT TO DO THIS OR NOT?

I GUESS SO...
YOU BETTER.
NO ONE GETS IN SIGMA CHI WITHOUT THE RITUAL. SET UP THE TALISMANS, NEOPHYTE.

I CALL UPON THEE RAGGINOR, KILLER OF TIME, ENTER THIS REALM AND FULFILL THE ...
...THIS IS DUMB.

I DON'T NEED YOUR CREEPY SORORITY AND ALL THIS GOTH CRAP. NONE OF THIS STUFF WORKS, ANY--

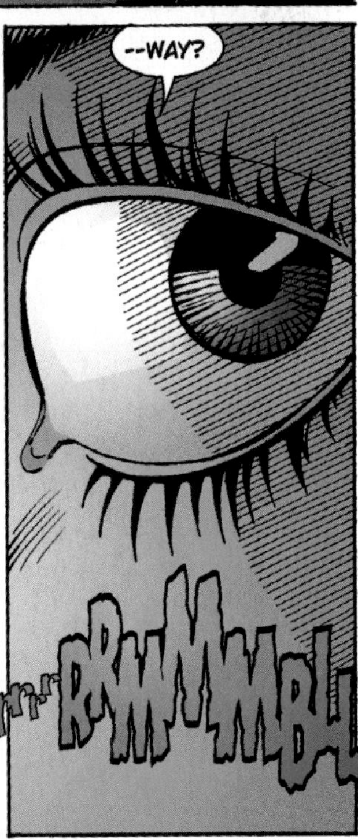
--WAY?
RRMMMBL

NOW.
>SIGH< LOOKS LIKE MY STOP.

GUESS THOSE GOTH GIRLS STOLE THE MUSEUM'S PENDANT TO UNLEASH MAJOR BADNESS. ONLY QUESTION IS--
Cher
Cola

OOOF! --WHAT KIND?
TELEPATH. SWELL.

HEY, BIG GUY! TELEPATHY TIP: IF YOU WANNA TAUNT ME? TRY ENGLISH, DORK!

SKKRASH
SILENCE, WHELP! NONE MAY MOCK RAGGINOR!

RAGGINOR, HUH?
THANKS FOR THE LIFT.

U.C. SUNNYDALE
DINGOES
Live
RRRING!

WILL? ME. WHAT DO WE KNOW ABOUT A DEMON NAMED RAGGINOR? I'M MORE THAN A LITTLE CURIOUS HERE.

RAGGINOR? OOH. BAD BOY. CONJURE HIM NEAR A CLOCK, HE TAKES FORM AT MIDNIGHT, AND, UH... ENDS ALL TIME AS WE KNOW IT.
FUN. HOW DO I SLAY HIM?
YOU CAN'T.

KRR-ATCH
HE'S AN ELEMENTAL. UNTIL HE INCARNATES, SLAYING RAGGINOR'D BE LIKE BEATING UP THE OCEAN. HE'S POWERFUL...

...BUT DUMB THINKS TH CLOCK IS TIM ITSELF. SO STO THE CLOCK..

...YOU STOP THE--
SHKNARK!
KRRASH!

--END OF ALL TIME. MAYBE.
11:58 PM

OKAY. BEAT THE CLOCK BEFORE DO-RAG TAKES FORM. PIECE OF CAKE.

DIE, SLAYER!
STALE, CRAPPY CAKE.

YOU CANNOT STOP ME, SLAYER!
KKRSSHH!

GONNA TRY.

PRAY TO YOUR GODS FOR MERCY! THE END OF TIME HAS COME.
HEY!
KEEP OUT

DEAL WITH YOU LATER.
I TOLD YOU WE SHOULD HAVE PLAYED YAHTZEE, BUT NOO...

WHOOF!

DO YOU NOT UNDERSTAND? I AM THE APOCALYPSE!

KREEEEAAA
MY POWERS ARE LEGION!

MY FORMS KNOW NO LIMITS!

YOUR HUMAN EFFORT SICKENS ME!

BEGONE!

AS RAGGINOR THE DESTRUCTOR TAKES FORM!

I AM RAGGINOR! THE END OF TIME! RULER OF ALL KNOWN REALMS! ANNIHILATOR OF THE--
YEAH, YEAH...
YOU FORGOT "CHUMP."
PSSS SSST
YAAAH!
AAAAHRRGGHHH!!!
KA-SHUNK!
SHLOOP
KANK
BUFFY! ARE YOU OKAY? WHAT HAPPENED TO RAGGINOR?
HIS TIME WAS UP.
SO THE END OF THE WORLD'S POSTPONED AGAIN. COOL. WHAT DO YOU WANT TO DO NOW?
I WAS THINKING OF PLAYING YAHTZEE...
THE END